a minedition book

published by Penguin Young Readers Group

Published simultaneously in Canada.

Manufactured in Hong Kong by Wide World Ltd.

Designed by Michael Neugebauer

Typesetting in Silentium Pro Roman designed by Jovica Veljovic

Library of Congress Cataloging-in-Publication Data available upon request.

Color separation by Fotoreproduzioni Grafiche, Verona, Italy.

ISBN 0-698-40000-3

10 9 8 7 6 5 4 3 2 1

First Impression

For more information please visit our website: www.minedition.com

Hans Christian Andersen tHE eMPEROR'S nEW cLOTHES

Re-cut, pinned and stitched
by John A.Rowe

MINeDITION

Once upon a time there was an Emperor who loved shopping and spent all of his money on new clothes. He didn't care about dancing at balls, going to the theatre, or riding in his carriage, unless he was able to show off his new clothes!

The Emperor was never found sitting on his throne because he spent all of his time shopping for new clothes. It took all of his servants to carry the many new things he would buy each day.

The city where the Emperor lived was a wonderful place. Many visitors came to see it. One day, however, two tricky rascals arrived in town, pretending to be weavers and claiming to make the most beautiful cloth anyone had ever seen. The clothes made from their cloth were so fine and delicate that they were invisible to anyone who didn't work hard at their job, or who was remarkably stupid.

"Those must be marvelous clothes indeed," thought the Emperor excitedly. "If I wore them, I would be able to tell who wasn't working hard at their job. I would also know who was stupid and who was clever. I must have that cloth made for me at once!" he decided. And the Emperor gave the two swindlers lots of money so that they would begin weaving their amazing cloth.

The swindlers immediately set up their loom. They asked the Emperor to provide the finest silk and the most precious gold thread in all the land, all of which they quickly hid away for themselves. And each day the two swindlers pretended to work late into the night at their empty looms.

Everyone was talking about the wonderful powers of the cloth. They were all eager to find out how clever or how stupid their neighbors were. All the talk made the Emperor curious. He wondered how his cloth was coming along. "I will send my best servant to see it. No one works harder than he and he is very clever. Surely he will be able to see the delicate cloth and report back to me."

So the Emperor's best servant went into the hall where the two swindlers were sitting at their empty loom. "This just can't be," thought the servant, opening his eyes as wide as possible. "I can't see the cloth! Surely, I am clever," he thought to himself. "Surely, I work hard enough carrying all of the Emperor's shopping bags. This just won't do. I won't tell anyone that I can't see the cloth."

"What do you think?" asked one of the swindlers as he pretended to weave.

"Oh yes. It's very nice indeed! Really splendid!" answered the servant, rubbing his eyes. "Yes, I will report to the Emperor that I like it very much!"

"Delighted to hear it!" said the two weavers as they continued to talk about the colors and the pattern. The servant listened carefully so that he could tell the Emperor all about it, and so he did.

Soon the Emperor couldn't think about anything but his new clothes. He began to get impatient.

The Emperor decided to send his hairdresser to see how the weaving was coming along and to find out if the cloth would be ready soon.

So the Emperor's hairdresser went into the hall where the two swindlers were sitting at their empty loom. Just as the servant before him, the hairdresser looked and looked, but he saw nothing on the loom. "This just can't be!" he thought to himself. "Surely, I am clever. Surely, I work hard enough combing and brushing the Emperor's hair. This just won't do. I won't tell anyone that I can't see the cloth."

"Isn't it a fine piece of cloth?" asked the two swindlers, as they pretended to show it to him, running their hands through the air as if stroking it.

"Yes indeed!" confirmed the hairdresser, reaching out to feel the quality of the cloth which wasn't really there. "I would love a hat made from it!"

"Yes, a hat would be wonderful," the two swindlers agreed.

Of course, the hairdresser returned to the Emperor and reported how beautiful the cloth was.

Now all the people in town were talking about the wonderful cloth. Well, the Emperor just couldn't wait any longer. He had to see the cloth for himself. He invited all of his helpers to join him. When they entered the hall, the two swindlers were weaving away with all their might, although there wasn't a single thread on the loom. "Isn't it superb?" said the servant to the hairdresser. And he pointed to the empty loom, believing that everyone else could see the cloth.

"Goodness me!" thought the Emperor. "This just can't be. I can't see a thing. Surely, I am clever. Surely, I work hard enough buying all my clothes," he thought to himself. "This is the worst thing that could possibly happen to me! I just won't tell anyone that I can't see the cloth." So the Emperor nodded approvingly at the empty loom and said, "Oh yes, it is beautiful! I like it very much indeed!"

All of his helpers stared and stared, but they couldn't see a thing either. But they all copied the Emperor's enthusiasm. "Superb! Exquisite! Excellent!"

They were all so pleased that they advised the Emperor to have the wonderful cloth made into a suit of clothes to wear in the great procession that would be taking place very soon. So the two swindlers appeared to work very hard to finish the Emperor's new clothes on time. They pretended to take the cloth off the loom. They snipped their scissors in empty air and they busily sewed using needles without any thread. Soon they announced, "Bring the Emperor, his clothes are ready!"

The Emperor arrived with all of his helpers. The two swindlers pretended to hold up the Emperor's new clothes. "Here they are," they said. "Perfectly you! And they are just as we expected—light as a feather and easy to wear. You will feel as though you are wearing nothing at all!"

The swindlers pretended to dress the Emperor in the new clothes they were supposed to have made for him, fitting them around his waist and acting as if they were tucking his ears in under his fancy new hat. Then the Emperor turned and bowed and walked proudly back and forth in front of the mirror.

Everyone agreed. "That's a splendid suit of clothes indeed!"

"I'm ready!" announced the Emperor excitedly as he danced and posed like a ballerina in front of the mirror one last time. As he left the room everyone clapped and cheered. The streets outside were overflowing with visitors, and flags were being waved from the windows. Cries of excitement filled the air as the Emperor appeared and made his way slowly along the street. "Oh, how wonderful the Emperor looks in his new clothes! How well they suit him!"

Comments continued from every direction. No one wanted to admit that they couldn't see anything, because that would have meant that they were stupid or that they weren't working hard enough at their job.

The Emperor felt wonderful in his new clothes, just as if he was wearing nothing at all! He was very proud. None of his other clothes had ever been so greatly admired.

All of a sudden, through all the cheers and cries, almost so quiet as not to be heard, a small child's voice said, "But the Emperor has no clothes on!"

Some of the visitors laughed. "How sweet, the poor child thinks the Emperor has no clothes on." Then, as each one looked again, they began to wonder and whisper to each other. "The Emperor has no clothes on!" Finally, everyone was shouting, "The Emperor has no clothes on!"

The Emperor began to feel very silly, because he knew that they were right. He really didn't have any clothes on!

But he was a good Emperor and he held his head even higher. He laughed out loud as he thought about how funny he must look. And everyone laughed with him. They continued to wave their flags and their cheers for their great Emperor became even louder.

Without hesitation, the Emperor made a royal bow, pretending to tip his hat, and declared this day a holiday. He called it...
The Emperor's No Clothes Day!